Meet Inspector
L. JACK HAWTHORNE

Meet Inspector
L. JACK HAWTHORNE

Justin P. DePlato

authorHOUSE®

AuthorHouse™ LLC
1663 Liberty Drive
Bloomington, IN 47403
www.authorhouse.com
Phone: 1-800-839-8640

Published by AuthorHouse   07/11/2013

ISBN: 978-1-4817-7372-0 (sc)
ISBN: 978-1-4817-7373-7 (e)

Library of Congress Control Number: 2013912114

To my Mother, for sharing with me the love of mystery.

CONTENTS

CHAPTER 1

Greetings from William Cleese

This is a story about the greatest inspector no one knows. I am probably the only friend Inspector Hawthorne has, and this is probably because Inspector Hawthorne is not a very likable guy. What I mean by unlikable is that Inspector Hawthorne is the very essence of a curmudgeon. You could easily say Inspector Hawthorne gave the word *curmudgeon* its definition, not the other way around. He is a very ornery man. Often after meeting Hawthorne, people leave his company feeling inadequate—by that I mean they feel stupid. He has an ability to make people feel small.

My friendship with the inspector started many years ago. To understand how our friendship started, first you need to know a little bit about me. I am Inspector William Cleese of the Royal Berkshire Yard. I am by no means famous, not even in Berkshire. Though, not to sell myself short, I did crack the infamous White Burger heist in 1943. Aside from that case, my job is pretty much catching small-time crooks who like to steal little old ladies' handbags or, from time to time, the bungling accidental murderer who practically falls in my lap.

Back to how I know Inspector Hawthorne. One of the first cases I worked on with Hawthorne happened back in 19 thing happened just north of Berkshire, in the small town of Hampton in the south of England. There was a murder—not just an ordinary, *oops* kind of murder; it was a big-deal kind of murder. The dead guy was none other than Wendell Holmes.

Holmes was a very rich man. His family owned the largest textile company in town and had amassed enough money to buy a private estate just outside the Hampton limits, on a parcel of the land the Holmes family claimed as their own. With little hesitation, they named the parcel after their family name: Holmes, England. For a rich guy, no one really knew anything about Wendell Holmes—a home body, he epitomized the true definition of a misanthrope. The only time he ever came into town was on Sunday for the Catholic service. One could say his Englishness fell short of ever being complete.

The murder took place on a Sunday, but not an ordinary Sunday. It was Easter Sunday. Easter is the day Christians celebrate the resurrection of their lord and savior, Jesus Christ, who, if my memory of the historical record serves me, was and is the only man to ever defeat death. In any event, it was Easter Sunday, 1944, when Wendell Holmes died in front of everyone, slumped over in his pew at the Hampton Cathedral.

How did the death of the miser Wendell Holmes lead to me meeting Inspector Hawthorne? I thought you might ask. Let me tell you. Hawthorne, who by any measure was not a religious man, was not in Hampton to celebrate Easter. He was in Hampton visiting his somewhat estranged brother, Timothy Hawthorne. I say "estranged" because Jack Hawthorne only saw his brother on holidays, and by holidays I mean Christmas and Easter. You might ask why only the religious holidays. The answer is because Timothy, Jack's big brother, was a devout Christian, as were Jack's late parents, Mary and Peter. And yes, Mary and Peter used to live in jolly old Hampton. They'd died several years earlier. Hawthorne would go back to Hampton to visit his brother and visit his parents' graves. So, needless to say, Jack only came to town to serve his filial and brotherly duties, not because he wanted to spend time in Hampton, and certainly not to attend church.

Strangely, though, Jack Hawthorne has an uncanny ability for being at the wrong place at the right time. He is, after all, an inspector—I think the greatest never known. Murder finds him like a dog finds a buried bone in the backyard. You can rest assured that when a murder took place in merry England, one that would be hard to solve, hard to fathom, Jack Hawthorne would already be in attendance—no need to call him. Somehow the forces of nature, maybe dark magic, had already added Hawthorne to the scene.

CHAPTER 2

Meeting Inspector Hawthorne

L et me tell you about the first time I met Inspector Hawthorne. The day was January 11, 1943, a cold, dark day in Amsterdam, Netherlands. I was visiting the city to attend a police expo (basically a fun gathering for inspectors, who, like most, think the world of themselves). I was attending to learn things about inspecting techniques and to see the city (I had never been to Amsterdam before).

The first day of the conference was when I met Hawthorne. I ran into him at a meeting—I mean I really ran into him. I was walking into the conference hall (a big old building, the new *museumplein*, with a large foyer). I had in my hand a delicious Dutch coffee—something to loosen me up a bit—and the daily London newspaper. As I entered the building, *boom*, I bumped into an oddly dressed man—Hawthorne.

Hawthorne was holding nothing. The man never drinks coffee, swears it makes him hyper and uncivil, like a raging bull. Apparently caffeine made Hawthorne more overtly irritable. He was wearing what I later came to know as a pretty normal outfit for him: a dark brown safari hat (to shield him from the pernicious rays of the sun), a blue tailored blazer, white button-down shirt, a bright red bow tie, and beige khaki pants. His shoes, classic winged-foot dress shoes, were blood red. The strangest thing about him, as if his dress were not strange enough, were his eyeglasses. His glasses were the sorriest pair I had ever seen. They were held together by tape, black tape, both at the conjoining nose appendage and on both frames over the ears. The things looked as if they had been through a personal brawl and yet somehow survived.

After I bumped into him, I stepped back to greet him. "Good day, sir," I said.

"Greetings," Hawthorne said with a slow-drawn pronunciation.

"I am sorry to run into you this way. I was walking too fast, drinking too fast, and trying to read, all at the same time—how silly of me."

Hawthorne looked at me, puzzled. He gave me a long squinting look, as if he thought I was strange. "I see."

Hawthorne was sometimes a man of very few words, but powerfully instructive of his feelings. I suspect in that moment that Hawthorne was irritated by my actions. Then he turned and walked away.

I stood there for a moment, thinking, *That is all he has to say, "I see"? What a peculiar man—what was he thinking about me?*

The day passed. The conference was boring, and then it was time for lunch. I went to the main dining hall to enjoy a classic Dutch lunch: roast beef sandwich with tomato and fresh-cut French fries. I went to sit down, but most tables were taken—the only room left was a table to the far right corner of the dining hall. There sat that strange fellow I'd bumped into earlier, Inspector Hawthorne. I thought, *Should I eat with him? Why not? He must be harmless.* So I went over and formally introduced myself. "Greetings again, sir. I am Inspector Cleese. May I join you for lunch?" A moment passed in dead silence. Hawthorne didn't even look up to acknowledge I was standing there; he just kept on eating what appeared to be an open sandwich of meat, cheese, and tomatoes. I stood there waiting for a response, slowly becoming agitated. Then, finally, he said, "Hello. I suppose if there is no room anywhere else, since there is room available at my table then yes, you may sit here."

"Okay, thank you," I said rather reluctantly. I sat down and then everything began. It was like a light bulb was quickly turned on. Hawthorne became very chatty.

"What brings you to Amsterdam and this conference? Are you an inspector?" Hawthorne asked.

"I am an inspector for the Royal Berkshire Yard—fourteen years of excellent service" I added.

"Well, that sounds wonderful. I am here because I am an inspector too, but I do not work for just one yard. Oh no—too simple, if you ask me. I work for the entire country of England—I am Inspector Hawthorne. You have probably heard of me or have read of me," he said boastfully.

I paused for a moment because I did recognize the name; however, I never knew the face. This was the famous Inspector Hawthorne, the same guy who caught the midnight London rapist, the Butcher of Bakersville. *I suppose it is true: the great ones are always weird and mysterious. This man sure is that.* "Pleasant to meet you, Inspector Hawthorne," I said. "I have certainly read about your detective genius. I admire you just as much as the rest of England—this is certainly a great moment to be in your presence."

"Thank you," Hawthorne said. "I often enjoy hearing how others have heard of me or, even better, admired me, but now I must go. I am needed to deliver a speech. Meeting you was pleasant—good day to you." Hawthorne stood up and simply walked away. I remembered that he was the featured speaker, so I hurried to hear him speak. After the conference I never saw him again until the two of us worked on a crime in Berkshire (but that story is for another time).

Now to Hampton, where Hawthorne and I were traveling to visit family and the unexpected detective work in investigating a murder.

CHAPTER 3

Off to Hampton

"Good morning, Jack. How are you on this gloomy morning?" I said.

"Greetings, William. I am doing fine this gloomy morning. I am excited to board the train and be on our way to Hampton," said Jack.

I thought for a second about traveling with Jack to Hampton. Jack was a peculiar person to travel with, because he had certain idiosyncrasies that made him at times unpleasant to be around. For starters, he always had to have the first cabin in the train, closest to the engine. Secondly, he always had to have a middle table in the dining cabin, and he required complete silence from 7 p.m. to 6 a.m. In the morning his breakfast had to be served promptly at 6:15. If any of these circumstances were not met, Jack became an intolerable person to be around, and the waiting staff would dread and despise ever knowing Jack Hawthorne.

Jack and I were sitting at a coffee shop table waiting for out train to depart. I was enjoying a short latte, while Jack was having his usual black Irish coffee and a small cheese Danish pastry. He was reading the *London Times* while I was working on a crossword puzzle. Often when the two of us sat anywhere, the conversation was limited—not because I did not want to talk but because Jack was a man of very few words, mostly coarse words when he did offer them. So talking to him was best when it was at a minimum. But in the course of a murder investigation, there was no other person I would rather talk to and listen to than Jack, because what he would say and know about an investigation was not just amazing, it was almost divine, sacred, out of this world, how quickly and insightfully he would figure out the murder puzzle.

"Jack, how is the coffee, is it strong enough for you?" I said.

Slowly looking up at me from his paper, his broken glasses falling to the tip of his nose, he answered, "William, the coffee is strong enough. If it wasn't I would not be drinking it. Must you bother me with such trivial and obvious questions? How many times must I tell you small talk, chit chat, chewing the fat, whatever you must call it, is for women; it is not for noble men, enlightened thinkers, of such rare form as ourselves. Now, if you wanted to ask me about the falling value of the pound or the latest fancy fandango invention, then we might have a conversation, but anything short of a worthwhile question should by all means be kept to yourself." He then looked back down to his paper, not caring if I responded.

"Of course, Jack, I often forget that you are not interested in the obvious. You are only interested in the unobvious," I said, puzzled by the last clause of my sentence—*will he correct my English, or just ignore it? Ah, who cares?* I thought to myself. I went back to doing my crossword puzzle.

The steam engine horn blew at approximately 7:15 a.m. noise to my ears. The horn meant we were about to board the train. When traveling with Jack the most common thought in my head was, "Let's get on with it." The faster we traveled, the faster we arrived—that was good, if you asked me.

Jack turned up from the newspaper and said, "Well, William, do we need to state the obvious or shall we just get up and make our way to the train?" Typical wisecrack humor from a very obstinate man. We both stood up, grabbed our bags, and made our way to the train. It was time to head off to Hampton to celebrate Easter with the Hawthornes.

CHAPTER 4

At Hampton

When we arrived in Hampton the gloom from Berkshire had not subsided. I think the amount of rain falling in Hampton actually topped Berkshire. I guess the old saying "Rain in Berkshire is worse than any" is actually not true. Nonetheless, Hawthorne and I had slept most of the train ride, and when the train stopped we were both very eager to get off the train and on our way. (Though it was a short ride south to Hampton, Hawthorne was an avid sleeper.)

Once we stepped off the train, Hawthorne and I grabbed our black travel bags from a very nice bellman and immediately hailed a black taxi cab. "Hawthorne, this way," I said. Hawthorne had an uncanny ability to walk in the wrong direction, generally away from the person he was with. He often appeared like a blind man, aimlessly wandering around.

"Ah, yes, William, I see you now. I am coming," Hawthorne said.

Once we were in the cab, off we went. Hawthorne and I sat quietly, each to our own devices. I was reading the *London Times* and Hawthorne was scribbling notes in his little red book. Hawthorne's little red book is the most unusual thing. He takes the book everywhere and never lets anyone see inside it. I often wonder just what on earth he has written inside that red book, yet I realize I will never know. Maybe after he is dead I could get my hands on it. I bet Hawthorne would simply burn the book before he died rather let anyone ever see it.

Hawthorne sat quietly doodling in his book, so I felt the need to inquire, "Hawthorne, what are you writing over there?"

Hawthorne slowly looked up from his book, his broken glasses falling down his nose. He peered over the glasses. "What does my writing matter to you? I am obviously working on some notes—things I need to mention to my brother while in town."

"Okay," I said.

The car abruptly stopped, ending our terse conversation. "Hawthorne estate, gentlemen," said the driver. Hawthorne and I stepped out of the car at Jack's family estate. What a beautiful place. The Hawthorne house was a classic Victorian estate with large beautiful grounds and a terrace. It was the most meticulous place I think I ever saw—surprising for Hawthorne, simply because he was a bit of a pack rat.

We stepped up the front steps, and Hawthorne's brother opened the door to greet us. "Greetings, gents, how are you?" said Timothy Hawthorne, Jack's younger brother.

"We are fine," replied Hawthorne. "Timothy, grab my coat. I need to get this wet dog off of me."

"Will do," replied Timothy. "Gents, come in, and let me get you some warm tea. I know you both like your tea with a pinch of cream. How about a nice tiny cake with it?"

"Sounds delicious," said William.

"Come. Why don't you sit down at the table, and I will get the tea and cake." Timothy strolled over to the counter, grabbed some tea cups, and began pouring the tea. Meanwhile, Hawthorne and I sat down at a small white round table and took a moment to relax. The train ride was long, and standing outside in the rain made us more tired. I looked around Timothy's small house. It was the first time I had been to Timothy's house. The house was decorated with many odd trinkets. Many of them appeared to be from antiquity, like Roman symbols of fertility or Jupiter, or Egyptian obelisks—even some fantastic Renaissance prints, many of which depicted the great stories of Christianity. There was a little piece of paper on the kitchen table with an odd sketch on it that struck my eye. On the paper, I thought I saw a circle enclosed in a square, dotted in the very center. I found the drawing strange, but since I was a guest I felt it was not my place to opine on the matter of the drawing (at least not yet).

"Gents, here is your tea and cake. So tell me, how was the train ride?" asked Timothy.

"Oh, the ride was very ordinary. We had a smooth, non-eventful trip from Berkshire. I spent most of my time reading, while William spent his time drawing or doing mindless crosswords," said Hawthorne. I jumped in to defend my work but was interrupted by Hawthorne. "So, Timothy, what are you up to these days? You know why I am in town, right?" asked Hawthorne.

"Of course I know why you are in town. You are here for Easter and to see the traditional Easter service, and of course to see Mom and Dad."

Traditionally, Hawthorne went to Hampton each Easter to visit his parents, his dead parents. He always laid tulips on their graves, fresh from Holland. He would kneel and whisper a quiet prayer and then be off to the service. The whole thing, coming from a rather dull curmudgeon, was very wholesome and nice.

"Well, Timothy, I dare say we'll ignore this strange drawing on your desk and make our way to the cemetery. Service does start at 11a.m. and I do not want to miss it."

"Okay," replied Timothy.

Off we went. The drawing was placed into Timothy's pocket, he grabbed his keys, and we were all off to the cemetery in the fanciest, red Rolls Royce I had ever been in. We didn't spend much time at the cemetery. Hawthorne placed the tulips at the site, presumably said a prayer, and then we were off to church.

CHAPTER 5

To Church

We set out for the church. Hawthorne was dressed in a black suit, wearing his broken, taped glasses and his usual black English cap. Timothy drove the car like a bat out of hell, yet somehow we made it to church, though a bit later than expected, just as the service was starting. We had little time to dawdle, so we headed right to our pew. We took a moment to shake the hands of the family that always sat behind, the Holmes family.

The Holmes family was very close to Jack, Timothy, and their parents. The Holmes were famous in town for their huge textile business. They were in the business of handcrafting suits. Their suits were the ones that the Hawthornes and everyone else in Hampton wore to church. Wendell Holmes, the patriarch, was an earnest, ornery man. He was a man of few words, but when he spoke, everyone listened. He had two sons, both being groomed to run the business once their frail, elderly father had expired.

Rex was the elder son. He looked nothing like his father. His father had bushy eyebrows, a permanent scowl on his saggy face, huge cheekbones, and minimal gray and white hair. Rex had dark, plush hair, combed precisely and with class and a bright, huge smile. He was the best-manicured man I had ever known. He wore suits, or any outfit, with panache.

Ben was the younger brother; he did not have his elder brother's good looks or charm. Ben was a prototype of Wendell. Ben never married, had never experienced the fondness of temporal pleasures, and the townsfolk always speculated that Ben resented his brother. When looking at the differences between the two, resentment was an obvious conclusion. Ben took a likely to the family business. He was Wendell's shadow and most obvious heir to the Holmes' fortune.

Rex, on the other hand, enjoyed the finer things in life, mainly women, wine, travel, and leisure. But although pursuing life's finer qualities, Rex had the smarts to know he still had to learn the business, and since he was the eldest, Rex always assumed he would inherit the family business.

Wendell's wife was the enchanting and often misunderstood Lady Holmes. I never learned her real name; I am sure it was something more than Lady, but everyone called her Lady, and so did I. She was a lady of great pride, humility, and compassion. For all the bitterness that Wendell possessed, Lady Holmes equaled his bitterness with kindness. I affirm to do this day I never heard Lady Holmes, even during the tragedy, ever speak ill about anyone. She was almost too nice, some might say. I know some writers will remind us that "even good people do bad things." This may be true, though many good people only do good things, and the latter, not the former, fit Lady Holmes.

Sitting across the aisle from the Holmes was the other great family in town, the Cartrights. Unlike the Holmes family, who were always in Hampton, a part of Hampton, and quite possibly the first family ever to live in Hampton, the Cartrights were originally from Dorchester. They'd moved to Hampton about a hundred years earlier, which seems like a long time, but in the history of Hampton and in the ways folks speak of the rivalry between the two families, you would think that a hundred years ago was like yesterday.

The Holmes despised the Cartrights, and vice versa. *Why?* you might wonder. Well, the Holmes family built the Rex Textile Industries. They manufactured everything from men's suits to ladies dresses to hats, socks, belts, and even undergarments. In the early twentieth century, finding an Englishman who did not wear something adorned on them from Rex Industries was practically impossible—until the Cartrights moved into Hampton.

Roger Cartright founded Cartright Textile Industries. You guessed it—the Cartrights manufactured everything the Holmes factories already produced, but the Cartrights did produce things a bit cheaper. This competition between the two manufacturers and two families continued for generations to the present day. Roger Cartright and W. Holmes Sr., the originally founders, were long dead, but the sons John Cartright and Rex and Ben Holmes (along with their father Wendell Holmes Jr.), now ran the businesses, respectively. Roger Cartright Jr., though, had died a year or two ago. Not one Holmes family member attended his funeral. So talk about adding fire to a wildfire. From that day forth Adeline Cartright, the wife of Roger Jr., vowed she would do everything in her power to undermine, destroy, or cripple the Holmes family and their business. Needless to say, a tornado was brewing between these two families—a collision course of unparalleled magnitude was casting shadows on beautiful Hampton. The folks were just waiting to see which shoe fell first.

Hawthorne turned to the pew behind him and shook Wendell Holmes's hand. Holmes looked tired and bewildered. He looked up, gazed forward, and shook Hawthorne's hand. "Good to see you, Rex. I am relieved to see you here today.'

Hawthorne had no idea what Wendell was talking about. He nodded politely, "Good to see you too, Wendell. Enjoy the service. Lady, always a pleasure to see you as well." He nodded his head.

Everything changed so quickly. Once the organ began to play, Lady Holmes let out a loud scream that the whole congregation could hear. "Oh, my God, what is wrong with Wendell?" Right behind Hawthorne, Wendell Holmes had slouched over in his seat, apparently passed out.

Lady Holmes was frantic. "Wendell, talk to me, talk to me, please come back!" Rex Holmes pushed his way to his father. "Dad, what is wrong? Talk to us." The whole church went silent.

Hawthorne turned around and gazed at a disturbing scene. Wendell had fallen completely over in his pew. Hawthorne and his intuition told him something was amiss. "Move aside," he declared. "Let me check his pulse." Hawthorne grabbed Wendell's wrist and felt the emptiness of death. "Lady, I am so sorry, but Wendell is dead."

The whole congregation gasped simultaneously.

"Are you sure?" exclaimed the exhausted Lady.

"Yes, yes, indeed—he is dead," quietly said Hawthorne.

A few moments later the police and ambulance were on hand. They confirmed what was already known. Easter Sunday service and Wendell Holmes, the patriarch of Hampton, had died in his pew. The question on everyone's mind now was, was it murder or old age? A quick autopsy would determine that answer. However, Hawthorne thought to himself that an obvious answer lay in front of them. Wendell was murdered.

CHAPTER 6

Meet the Killer

On a damp evening in Hampton the killer slowly planned his attack. He knew that in order to kill Wendell Holmes he had to be smart, cunning, and crafty. After all, the entire town would be on the hunt for the person who killed their beloved Wendell. He thought for two hours, sitting at his oak desk, about just how he should kill the man he despised. Since boyhood he had dreamed about killing the old man who had ruined everything for him. He despised his hair, his grin, his walk, his money, and most of all his unfounded arrogance. So the killer, thinking about killing Wendell, thought, *What joy*!

First he thought he would shoot the old bird, but that would be messy, loud, and leave too many clues. Second, he thought about kidnapping the old bird and torturing him a bit before killing him, but alas, like the first option, such a remedy would be too risky for protecting himself. Finally, the solution dawned on him. *Poison. They will never detect the poison, and if they do, they will never realize the administration, or the technique used.* Unless he framed someone else. *Perfect,* he thought in his sinister mind. *I will kill the old bird using poison, but where and when?* The answer hit in the head like a shovel barreling down on him. *Church! What a perfect place to kill a man of God*, he thought. The plan now was certain—go to church, poison Wendell, and have revenge.

The killer smiled with the ugly face of anger—sinister, hostile anger. He took his pen and began to write out the plan and a loosely written letter. Time was of the essence, so he quickly departed for Hampton to purchase the poison and to stake out the church.

CHAPTER 7

Let the Investigation Begin

As the coroner took Wendell's body away, Jack Hawthorne quickly went into detective mode. He knew that every second mattered in detective work. Every clue, every look, every word was of paramount importance if he was going to catch the cold-blooded murderer. Jack Hawthorne believed that murders only happened for three reasons: one, out of hatred; two, out of despair; or three, because of money. He believed when someone hated a person or an outcome, he or she would possibly turn to crime. Men or women who had fallen out of or in love or experienced significant betrayal in their life, according to Hawthorne, were always more susceptible to crime, and those who desired money but were excluded from it were easily intoxicated by the thought of crime. Those would be the motives, he thought. Now he had to figure out which motive was correct and which person would have reason to kill.

Hawthorne began by surveying the crime scene. Wendell lay dead, slouched over in his pew; to the left of him was the aisle; to the right of him was Wendell's wife, Lady Holmes. Hawthorne had been sitting right in front of Wendell and was a witness himself to the apparent murder—he knew nothing strange had happened, no strangle, no noise, no clutter. All of sudden Wendell collapsed and was dead.

Because the killing was so silent, Hawthorne immediately suspected poison as the means. He knew that an autopsy would possibly reveal such a method; evidence of the poison would appear underneath the fingernails, leaving no doubt of poison as the weapon. But the apparent question then was who poisoned Wendell and why? And how? Hawthorne recalled that when he shook Wendell's hand to greet him that morning, he looked lethargic and tired. He didn't recall Wendell drinking anything right before he collapsed. So when was the poison administered to Wendell, and how?

Hawthorne was a student of toxicology and anything crime related, so he wisely knew that some poisons were slow killers, similar to a python wrapping around their prey. He knew the administration of the poison could have happened earlier, but if so, who did it and why?

"William, come look at this," ordered Hawthorne.

"What is it?" I replied. We both starred down at a very tiny object lying beneath Wendell's pew. The object was shiny, with a small encryption on it—two triangles fixed as a hexagon with a small dot in the center. Hawthorne immediately recognized the symbol as Masonic but wondered where it came from and why it was there. Did the killer leave the clue, or did Wendell? Or someone else?

I looked at Hawthorne. "What do you think? Do you think the object means anything about the murder?"

"Of course the object is important, William. Remember, nothing happens by chance in life. All actions are the predicate of motivation, and motivation is the predicate of will or desire. An object sitting underneath a pew where a man just died is undoubtedly important. Not only is the object important, but so might be the placement—whether it is right side up, or down, or even the fixed position. Is it pointing north, south, et cetera? All things have importance; it is our job to figure them out. Remember the Willowbrook killings? We found the strangest black button, and everyone at the crime scene figured the button was just a leftover piece of debris. However, the button was the most important clue, not because it had obviously fallen from the assailant but because the button told us a story about the killer and the killing because the button laid a certain way and pointed in a certain direction. Even the smallest, most benign object could offer the clearest, most important information we have when investigating a murder. Hence, the Masonic object is not just an object. Instead it may be the biggest clue we have about why Wendell is dead and how he was killed."

"I don't disagree with you, Hawthorne," I replied. "You are the best investigator for a reason, and that is because you solve mysteries that are usually deemed unsolvable. So what do you think the object means?"

"William, do not be hasty, I am not a soothsayer. I cannot just look at something and absorb its history or see how the object came to rest where it rests. I have no idea what it means now, but rest assured, when this case is solved we will look back at this little object and realize she also had the answers. The truth always stares right at us, yet we often have such a hard time seeing it, my friend. The truth is always revealed; that is why we keep trudging forward."

Hawthorne put the object in his pocket, and we went off to the Holmes' estate. We both knew that in order to find Wendell's killer we had to start with investigating the family and workers. After all, most crime are crimes of passion, the result of family struggle or employee/employer issues. We knew the answer to this riddle, the person who killed Wendell, lay not in the House of God but at home in the Holmes' house.

CHAPTER 8

To the Holmes Estate

The Holmes family made their money in the textile industry. You would be hardpressed to find a pair of slacks in all of England that were not Holmes produced. The family made a fortune clothing England. As such, they were very well known throughout England, but this was especially true in Hampton. The Holmes family built Hampton. You could not move around Hampton without seeing something related to the Holmes family, mostly things paying tribute to the family for building a business that built Hampton.

Like all families, the Holmes family was not perfect. There was clear sibling rivalry between the brothers and a mother who always tried to keep the peace. And of course Wendell had a favorite son—what father doesn't? But amazingly the Holmes family stayed together, avoided scandal, and retained a very positive public persona, even though most knew there was personal in-fighting (very similar to the royal family). So when the town learned of the murder, one might say everyone in town was shocked.

"Who would kill such an ornery man? I bet the killer was his son—he always wanted his money," the townsfolk opined. There was no doubt that people in those parts knew the effects of money on human emotion. Even in a tight-knit family, money and greed could cause malice.

Hawthorne and I pulled up to the Holmes mansion and were greeted by the family butler, Harold Shank. The family called him Harry. He was quite a nice man and a very jovial man, as well as a very astute butler. "Greetings, gents. I wish you were coming to visit on better terms, but nonetheless, you are our guests, and we will do whatever is necessary to accommodate and make your time with us as pleasant as possible. Come this way, if you please," Harry said. Harry took us through the grand entrance and foyer of the house and up the majestic staircase. Our room was the first on the left, a luxurious, grand old room, filled with all the modern comforts. We didn't rest long, Hawthorne was a very impatient man, so off we went to interview the possible suspects at large.

"Come on, William. We do not have all day to just sit around staring aimlessly at the walls. We have a murder to investigate, one that we must solve quickly, before the ever-elusive killer is out of our grasp. I fret that our killer is not one we will easily suspect. So we need to figure things out quickly and with great ease, as to not tip our hand too soon."

"Okay, okay. I am not delaying things, just trying to settle in. I will come with you," I said.

We immediately went downstairs to the main sitting room, where Lady Holmes was sitting alongside her youngest son, Ben. They were grieving over the loss of their father and husband. Lady Holmes was crying with intense sadness. Ben and Rex's eyes shared similar tears and redness. Standing to the back of the room was Mary Margaret, Lady Holmes's maid.

"Gentlemen, do come in and make yourselves comfortable. Mary, come fetch these fine men a hint of tea," said Lady Holmes.

"Gentlemen, how do you take your tea? Please come in and sit down," said Mary.

"Oh, just a spot of cream for me," said Hawthorne.

"A pinch of cream for me," I said.

"Lady Holmes, I am troubled and so sorry for the recent developments. I know you must be very distraught over the death of your husband. Trust me, I will solve this crime and bring this cold-blooded killer to justice. I sense he is among us, in this house, and I am positive that the clues necessary to bring him to justice will reveal themselves shortly. As they do I will see the whole puzzle of Wendell's death unfold in front of me," Hawthorne declared.

"Oh, I am so happy and confident that you will figure this whole mess out, Jack. Wendell always spoke so kindly of you and your family, especially your brother."

"My brother? I did not know that Wendell and Timothy were friends. Timothy never spoke of Wendell."

"Oh yes, Wendell and Timothy seemed to meet regularly, maybe monthly or so," said Lady Holmes.

"Hmm, interesting," muttered Hawthorne.

"I think they were friends at the Lodge," Ben chimed in. "In fact, I think they were both Lodge members. But they did do things outside the Lodge, and I would attest that Dad definitely enjoyed the company of your brother. I am sure Timothy will stop by to pay his respects," said Ben.

"Well, it is good to know that Wendell was a Mason. It might help explain some of the odd trinkets I discovered already. Just pieces of the puzzle coming into place," said Hawthorne. "Let me ask you a few questions, Lady Holmes, if you do not mind."

"Okay, just not too many," said Lady.

"First, did Wendell have any enemies that you knew of"?

"Not that I can think of, except for the obvious feud with the Cartrights. I do recall just a night or so ago hearing Wendell, I think, on the phone with Lady Cartwright arguing over something, probably business."

"I see," said Hawthorne.

"I heard that argument too," exclaimed Ben. "I think the conversation had to do with more than just business. I remember hearing Dad slam the phone down and muttering something to effect of 'She will never get it, never—I say never.' "Then I heard him write something down and turn off the light."

"Interesting," said Hawthorne, his brain working in overdrive. Just as I thought we would be sitting for awhile, Jack jumped up and said, "We must head upstairs, right away. I need to see Wendell's office," Hawthorne announced. So off we went, leaving Lady and Ben behind. Mary was kind enough to lead the way.

CHAPTER 9

Wendell's Office

We walked into Wendell's office, and we found a very organized, museum-like setting. Everything in the office was arranged neatly, with purpose, and orderly. Wendell's oak wood desk had some loose papers upon it; the chair was pushed out toward the main window, and the bookshelf had just one book missing from the hundreds spread across the shelves.

As Hawthorne and I entered the room, we were quickly greeted by Inspector Lewis. "Greetings, gents. I am glad to see you have come to the office. I have been waiting for you both."

"Hello, Inspector Lewis. I wondered if you would show up," said Hawthorne. "Have you found anything amiss here in the office?"

"Well, the loose papers on the desk are strangely ordered and are on a strange topic." We moved over to the desk and looked at the loose papers. The one sitting immediately in view was a loose small index with the following written on it: TEMPUS FUGIT; two other papers were neatly piled and had written on them SEMPER FIDELIS and CAVEAT HOMO. Hawthorne knew the meanings of each phrase: Always Faithful, Beware Man, and Time Flies, but neither of us understood why Wendell insisted on us knowing these phrases. We all looked at the writings and were puzzled.

Then Inspector Lewis informed us of the missing book. "The only other oddity in the room is the missing copy of apparently Wendell's favorite book, which is the Bible."

"Really?" said Hawthorne. "These strange writings, and his missing bible—how strange indeed.

"Of course there must be a reason behind all of this. That is our job to surmise, but what are your initial thoughts, Inspector Lewis?" asked Hawthorne.

"Well, I think we have ourselves a murder for money here. I think someone in the immediate family murdered Wendell to protect their inheritance, and I think that someone very close to Wendell tried to complicate the murder by staging a strange order of things, here in his office, to throw us off the chase," said Inspector Lewis.

"Indeed, I think you are right about the money, but I think all that we see here in the office was Wendell's doing. We could easily corroborate the handwriting with his family. I think Wendell left us clues about his murder—and murderer. I spoke briefly with his servant, and she recalled Wendell arguing just the night before his death with one of the sons over the estate. We need to interview her more thoroughly about her story, along with the other immediate family members, to determine the dynamics of the inheritance and why killing Wendell now would be so critical in protecting the family fortune," said Hawthorne. "I think it is quite clear that everything in this office offers clear evidence to point us to the killer. Our investigation will put all the pieces of this puzzle together, and when that does happen, then what appears as random fodder will turn out to be the most obvious of clues," Hawthorne surmised.

CHAPTER 10

The Suspects

Hawthorne immediately turned and left the room in a hurry. Clearly the old boy was on a mission—a mission to find the killer. Down the stairs he went and then off into the lobby, where he ran into Mary Margaret, servant to Mrs. Holmes.

"Greetings, dear Mary, how are you today?" said Hawthorne, slightly out of breath from his swift walk down the stairs.

"I am okay. I am saddened by Mr. Holmes death, of course. But I know that you will find out who did this to him," said Mary.

"Indeed I will. Now let me ask you a few questions, if you are up to it, dear Mary," said Hawthorne. "I recall you telling me when I first arrived here that the night before the deceased died you overheard Mr. Holmes talking with someone on the phone. And you mentioned the call was a bit harsh. Could you elaborate on the details of what you heard?"

"Well, I remember Mr. Holmes took the call around 11 p.m. I remember this because he had just had his single malt scotch, and he always had that drink around 11 p.m. Then he went into his study and took the call. At first there was little noise at all, but then suddenly Mr. Holmes began screaming, or I should say yelling, into the phone. I heard him say something to the effect of 'You will never be in charge, never'. Then he hung up the phone and called me into to turn down his bed," said Mary.

"And where was Mrs. Holmes?" asked Hawthorne.

"She was downstairs in the kitchen. I doubt she heard the call."

"Did Mr. Holmes say anything else to you?" asked Hawthorne.

"He did mention a strange thing. He looked at me and said, 'Hebrews and a Hebrew he is'. I had no idea what he meant, and then he laid down on the bed. I left and went downstairs to tend to Mrs. Holmes."

"Thank you, Mary—very good information," said Hawthorne.

"All right, William, we must go now and write out a list of suspects. I think we know Mrs. Holmes and the boys must be included. We must talk to them at once about the strange death of Mr. Wendell Holmes and ask who is this Hebrew we are looking for."

Hawthorne turned hastily to the kitchen to go and find Mrs. Holmes. Interviewing her about her husband's death would be difficult, but he knew she was hiding something about the mysterious death. As we entered the kitchen we ran into Mrs. Hawthorne standing over her chef complaining about the poultry lunch she was served.

Hawthorne quietly attempted to interrupt her argument. "Mrs. Hawthorne, could I have a minute or two with you? I don't mean to bother, but I have a pressing question to ask you."

Mrs. Holmes gazed at Hawthorne with her heavy brown eyes. She turned her head away from the shaking chef and turned to face Mr. Hawthorne. "Mr. Inspector Hawthorne. I am obviously dealing with a problem here, yet you still find it appropriate to interrupt me. I suppose your interruption is appropriate, because as you say your matter is very pressing. So, yes, I can spare a minute or two." Looking at the chef she quietly murmured something and then walked past us toward the sitting room.

"Come on, you two. Let's go sit down and rest for a moment. I am having Mary bring us some soothing gin. You care for some? Good. Now, let's enjoy a short time together as we discuss this awful event. I do hope neither of you will press me with gory details of the death or assume horrible premises about me, my husband, or my relationship with my husband," Mrs. Holmes said. As she outlined the parameters of the interview I could see Hawthorne's lip trembling. I knew he wanted to say something rude and pressing back to Mrs. Holmes, but in this moment he was polite.

"Dear Mrs. Holmes, of course we will not supersede our boundaries. Our questions will be cordial, polite, but of course necessary. So let me begin with a very simple question. Did you see, hear, or notice any unusual behavior from your husband the night before, or the morning of, his death?"

Mrs. Holmes sat back in her chair, as if she was put out by a difficult question. "Not that I can think of. My husband was a very ordered, religious, humble, and strong man. He did everything the same way, all the time. The night before the murder he took a call in the study and then he went to bed. I met him in bed around 11:15 p.m., and he seemed normal to me. The next morning he woke up around his usual 6 a.m. time; he went downstairs and waited for me to have breakfast around 6:30 a.m. I am unsure what he did for those thirty minutes. I always assumed he read the paper. You know how men are with their insatiable need for the news. Very tiresome behavior, if you ask me. We ate our usual egg breakfast. We finished around 7 a.m. He then went to his study. I went into the sitting room to plan the day with Mary. Oh, now that I am pressed to think about that horrid day, there was something odd about him at breakfast."

Hawthorne jumped in quickly. "Do tell, Mrs. Holmes. We need to know everything."

"Wendell said something odd to me as he went up the stairs to his study. He was also moving much slower than usual. I even made a point of mentioning his lethargic movement. He simply said his back was bothering him. But his movement was very strange indeed. Oh, and he did fuss a bit more than usual about pouring his coffee himself. In fact, he insisted on going into the kitchen to do so. Very strange, now that I think of it."

"Mrs. Holmes, good, good. But what about what he said to you as he went up the stairs?" I asked.

"Oh yes. He murmured something very strange. He said, 'Lady'—that is what he called me. 'Hebrews, they are all Hebrews'. I stood there and just said okay. Then he went upstairs."

Hawthorne was very puzzled by the news Mrs. Holmes shared. Mr. Holmes was lethargic, insisted on pouring coffee himself, and then murmured the strange comment about Hebrews. I was puzzled as well. What did all of this information mean about the killing of Mr. Holmes? We both knew that the murder weapon had to be poison, but when was the toxin administered, and by whom?

"Thank you, Mrs. Holmes," said Hawthorne. "William, let's go back upstairs to the study. We need to speak to the inspector and then find Mr. Holmes's sons. I think we are clearly aware of something now. Come on, we must hurry."

We hustled up the stairs to the study. Inside was the Inspector Lewis. "Gents, I have been looking for you. Where have you been? I think we have a very important clue here," said Inspector Lewis.

"We were meeting with Mrs. Holmes, but what is the clue?" said an excited Hawthorne.

"I found this little piece of paper inside this club jacket hanging behind the door." The jacket was the family club jacket, blue, with the embroidered *H* on the left side.

"What does the paper say?" asked Hawthorne.

"Well, the paper has just the following on it—15:11-32. A bunch of numbers. We have no idea of their meaning so far," said Inspector Lewis.

Hawthorne looked puzzled by the numbers. "Hmm, I guess we need to sit and think about this. Did you notice a bible sitting on the corner of the desk? Let's take a look inside that bible." We opened the bible. The book was last opened to Luke, chapter 15 verses 11-32. I figured Holmes must have been reading this scripture the night before his untimely death. The verses were the famous prodigal son story.

"Interesting that Wendell left us this clue about the prodigal son. Yet which of the Wendell boys is the prodigal son, and what does this mean? Consider this clue along with the earlier one about the Latin phrases and the strange hexagon. I am starting to think we do not know much about Mr. Holmes. Maybe he was part of an ancient religious order. Clearly Mr. Holmes was trying to tell us something. But Inspector Lewis, I think two more things are known, before considering these clues. One, I am positive poison killed Mr. Holmes and that the poison was given at breakfast the morning of his death. Two, I think that jacket is very important. In fact, I surmise the owner may be the killer.

Further, this strange bottle in the inside flap may be the poison bottle. I suggest you go and test this, Inspector."

"I agree with you, Mr. Hawthorne. We are already searching for the owner of the coat. We think the owner is Ben Hawthorne, because the inscription inside is *B*. We will find him and then ask him many questions."

"Good," said Hawthorne. "But we must now go and find Rex Hawthorne; I suspect he may know something about this death and maybe about these mysterious numbers. Let's go, William," said a hurried Hawthorne.

We hurried to the front foyer and asked Mary if she knew where Rex was, but she insisted that Rex had already left and returned to his house, which was kittycorner to the main house of the estate. So Hawthorne and I quickly put our jackets on and hustled to the door. As we were approaching the door, a gentleman briskly entered.

"Gents, I am glad to run into you. I am Franklin Sidmore, the family's lawyer. I came as quickly as I could, within good timing for this most unfortunate event. I am the purveyor of the will. Given that a day has passed since the killing, I figure it's time to read the will to the family. However, I could not find Rex, nor Ben; the sons must be present for the reading. Do you know where they might be?"

"Actually, we were looking for them as well. We were about to head off to Rex's house, though I surmise you have already tried there," I said. Hawthorne was clearly growing impatient with the boring conversation of idle nonsense, or should I say the lack of knowing anything about what the next step was.

"Gents, I doubt the boys wish to miss the reading of the will, so I suggest we sit down here and wait for them. I suppose they both know that there is a will, and I suppose both would want to know what they are entitled to, so I think it is fair to say that if they know Mr. Sidmore is here, they will arrive shortly, with great curiosity, for the reading of the will. In the meantime, why don't we have a short conversation Mr. Sidmore about the circumstances of this family estate, if you are able to answer any questions," Hawthorne suggested.

"I would rather hesitate to answer any questions until after the reading. Though I will tell you this. Mr. Holmes changed the will just five days ago, on very short notice. He called my office, which of course is in London, and insisted that over the phone I change some major components of the will. I did what he asked of me and asked no questions, but I must say I was surprised by the changes."

"What was Mr. Holmes's tone or urgency like?" asked Hawthorne.

"He was very hurried; he sounded irritated and had no interest in small talk. So I moved quickly on his request," said Mr. Sidmore.

Just as we were turning to sit down in the front sitting room, the front door swung briskly open. Two men stepped in. We assumed they were the Holmes boys; they bore striking resemblance to their father. Ben was a tall, thin, well-groomed boy. He wore impeccable business clothes: a tweed jacket, a striking red tie, and a fitted chapeau. His brother Rex was a bit more cavalier. He wore fancy slacks and a fitted polo shirt, with a sport jacket, no tie.

"Gents, sorry we were not here sooner. Ben and I were out back tending to some family business," said Rex. "I hope we can sit down and discuss the matters of the estate."

"Good to see you, Mr. Sidmore," said Ben.

"No rush, gents, we were just about to gather everyone together," said Mr. Sidmore. "Let's have Mary gather the house up, and we will begin the reading of the will."

Mary, who had been standing in the room quietly listening, quickly exited to gather the members of the household. First came Lady Holmes, looking stoic and bothered by the gathering. Then entered Harold Shank, the family butler, followed by Mr. Perch, the groundskeeper, Roger Lew the family accountant, and Rev. John Smith. Rex and Ben were already in the room, along with Hawthorne and me, anxiously waiting to here the news of the will. We both figured that the information in the will would help us understand the motive behind the killing—money is a catalyst for perilous events. Whoever got the most would most likely be more inclined to cause more peril—at least I thought so. Before the reading started Inspector Lewis popped in.

"Gents and ladies, thank you for gathering so promptly. Obviously the last day or so has been difficult for all of you. The passing of Mr. Holmes is a tragic event, not only for your family but also for this great town. As Mr. Holmes's lawyer I have the unkind task of going over this will with you. So, unless there are hesitations or questions, I suggest we move forward," said Mr. Sidmore.

There were no questions, but eyes were curious. Mr. Sidmore took out the will and opened the document. He glanced over the document and then said, "Gents and ladies, as you know, Mr. Holmes was a very kind man, but a mysterious man as well. I think you all knew this, but possibly not. Mr. Holmes requested some changes to the will a few short days ago; one that was very immediate was the time and place of the reading of the will. He insisted to me that I introduce the will here at the family estate but insisted that I irritate you by announcing that the reading of the will must take place in London at St. Paul's Cathedral. It disappoints me to have this task."

We all sat in shock, especially the family members. Everyone must have been thinking, *Read the will at St. Paul's? Why?* I turned to Hawthorne, and he appeared not surprised at all. "William, I already bought our tickets to London."

I was shocked. "Hawthorne, why did you buy tickets to London?"

"I obviously knew we were headed there. Not that I wanted to go, but I realized Mr. Holmes had more turns on this path for us to figure out, and clearly London was the next stop on our journey."

I couldn't figure out how Hawthorne came to know we had to head to London before being told, but that was part of the mystery of Jack Hawthorne. He just had a keen sense of knowing things. The boys and Lady Holmes were not happy at all, but that didn't surprise Hawthorne.

"I can't believe the old boy has us traveling to hear who gets what and why," said Lady Holmes.

"I know, Mother. Father was a man of mystery and intrigue. I guess this is only part of his final story," said Ben.

"Well, off to merry ole London, I suppose," said Rex. The boys then left to get ready. Lady Holmes departed upstairs with Mary to pack. Inspector Lewis left the room to make travel plans, and Mr. Sidmore took a deep breath and sat down. Hawthorne and I sat with him. Hawthorne turned to me and said, "I think before we head to London we should talk with Ben and Rex. Get a sense of their goings-on before the murder. I suspect the two of them know more than they are telling anyone. Though they seemed shocked to hear they had to head to London, as they prepared to go they did not seem put out by the change of the venue for the will reading. So either they are great thespians or they are soothsayers. Either or, we must know which it is," said Hawthorne. Hawthorne and I excused ourselves and headed into the dining room to meet with Rex and Ben.

CHAPTER 11

Interviewing the Holmes Boys

As we entered the kitchen, we both marveled at the fanciness of the room. Everything in the kitchen was in perfect order, from the pots to the pans to the linens to the perishables. The kitchen was a testament to efficiency and order. Just like every other room in the house, the kitchen was a perfect room. The Wendell boys were sitting at the service table enjoying a cup of coffee and talking with the head butler, Harold Shank. Hawthorne and I slowly and respectfully made our way over to the gentlemen.

"Gents, excuse us, but we were hoping to sit and chat a bit over the dealings of this sad affair. Would you permit us to have a short conversation with you?" asked Hawthorne.

"Yes, yes, no problem at all, though we do need to prepare for our travel in a bit, so we do not have all afternoon," said Ben.

"Great, just a few quick questions for you. Could you tell me anything you can recall from the night before the murder two nights ago?" asked Hawthorne.

Ben jumped in to answer first. "I was at my residency most of the night. I did talk with my father around 7 p.m., shortly after his 6:30 dinner. We just chatted about the function for Easter and then discussed some business matters, mainly a textile problem with a vendor out near Salisbury. Our conversation was short. I remember Dad said something about having to address some matters with Mom and that he would see me in the morning for church. That is all I recall from that evening," said Ben.

"Good, good," said Hawthorne. "And what about you, Rex—what can you recall from that evening?"

"Well, I was at the house for dinner; my wife Sarah and I had dinner with my parents. Over dinner we discussed mostly the Easter plans. Nothing too exciting, I must say. My father and I retired after dinner to the smoking room and enjoyed some of his favorite brandy and a cigar. We discussed the upcoming rugby match and argued over whether Liverpool could finally beat Fletcher. Sarah had some conversations with my mother, and then around 8 p.m. or so, we left for our home. My father was rather short and to the point most of the night. I do recall him acting tired, but nothing really out of the ordinary," said Rex.

"Was your father at all pale, or forgetful?" asked Hawthorne.

"I don't think so. I mean, for his age. He always looked pale and always forgot things—why do you ask?" said Rex.

"I think your father was poisoned, and I think the poison may have been given to him that evening. If I am right, then lethargy, paleness, and ambivalence would be part of the symptoms of the toxins," said Hawthorne.

"Well, you certainly do not think I gave him a toxin that evening! Such a claim is outrageous. I loved my father dearly. Yes, we did not always see eye to eye on things, but my father and I were compatible mates, if you will," said Rex.

Hawthorne, realizing he had hooked Rex the way he wanted, quickly rebutted. "Oh, I don't suspect you had anything to do with the poisoning, and I am impressed to hear of your devotion for your father, even if I didn't inquire into it. I think we have a clear case here of a man killed for his money, killed with the intent of hiding the truth behind the murder, hence the poison. I am unsure if the poison was administered the night before or the morning before, though after your thoughts, I suspect the poison was administered in the morning, at his normal breakfast time, with Lady Holmes present. And I certainly do not suggest Lady Holmes had anything to do with this unfortunate event, but her recap of the events leads me to strongly conclude that was the moment in time when said poison became relevant," said Hawthorne.

"Fair enough. I think I need to get my stuff together, so please do excuse me and my brother," said Rex.

"Good, I look forward to seeing both of you in London. I think our time in London will only help us figure the killer out," said Hawthorne.

The boys left, and Hawthorne and I finished our coffee. "William, I think London will have all the answers to this crime. Why Wendell is dead, who killed Wendell, and what the will reveals—all will be answered in London. The numbers from his office, the missing bible, and the location at St. Paul's Cathedral all point to a man trying to tell us something. What he is telling us is still a mystery, but I think we can clearly surmise that Mr. Holmes is talking to us from the grave—either to reveal the killer to us or to play with our intellect. Either is fine with me. I guess we should gather our things and head to the train station. Dreary London is waiting for us."

CHAPTER 12

Off to London-St. Paul's

H awthorne and I boarded the northbound train to London. Hawthorne was dressed in his usual suit, with a striking red tie. He had his favorite hat on, a striking gentleman's black hat. Of course his glasses were still fettered by a weird combination of string and tape. If I recall correctly, his glasses were actually older than he was. I thought they would easily fall off his face, yet they never did; instead they clung to his eyebrows and nose like a man clinging to a mountain wall for dear life.

The train was not full, nor busy. We were sitting in the luxury cabin. Hawthorne always traveled in style. He insisted on never sparing an expense when traveling. In fact, I think he overspent and outdid most prudent expenses when traveling. We took seats in the middle of the cabin. The Holmes boys took seats not too far from ours, and Lady Holmes took a seat about six seats away from ours.

Hawthorne quickly went off to his cabin, I was sure to organize and order the cabin to his fancy. I went off to my cabin and sat and read the *Times*. After a few short minutes there was a knock at my door. "Yes, who is it?" I asked.

"William, this is Ben Holmes. I need to speak with you at once." I was surprised to hear from Ben Holmes, so I hastened and opened the door.

"Ben, this is certainly a surprise. Come in at once. What is the matter?" I asked.

"Thank you for letting me in so easily, Mr. Cleese. I am sure you are bothered by the affairs of my family, and I am even sure that this trip is quite the bother, but I thank you for partaking in this unusual journey. You see, my father was a very odd man, but a good man. I would never harm him, nor would anyone in the family. That is why this whole state of affairs confuses and befuddles me. See, my father was a quiet man who only spoke when necessary and was all about business, night and day. He would not tire from work; he loved work. I must admit that I think this whole affair is about the family business—of that I am almost sure. Hence, my visit to you; you must realize that I am not one to surrender information about my family so easily, but I am very concerned about one thing, so much so that I will not just surrender it, I will offer it to you."

"Go on," I said, rather enthusiastically.

"My brother, Rex, and my father did not get along, especially when it came to the business. In fact, I know my brother had the worst of intentions for our business.

He wanted to sell the business, liquidate everything and live his life free from the doldrums of day-to-day work. I disagreed with him, but my father did more so. So much so that my father was rightfully consumed with preventing Rex from ever owning the business. But my brother was not a simpleton when it came to business. He knew that my father would have to bequeath the estate and would most likely do so to his wife or the sons, equally. Plus, my brother knows the law and was always prepared to enact power of attorney provisions or estate restrictions on the business to maintain leverage over my father's simple desire to pass the business to my mother and I. Plus, my mother has always favored Rex, so my father had a rightful concern that my mother would just give the business to Rex at some point. Needless to say, my brother is a shark, a shark who wanted to devour my father's real love, his business."

"Indeed, I see that this affair of business, family, and death was complicated," I retorted.

"Yes. I need you to know to watch out for my brother. He is not to be trusted. I am pretty sure he is responsible for this whole mess. My father was becoming quite senile, and I was sure my brother at some point would seize on my father's frailty to gain control over the estate, hence bypassing the will. I am surprised he would plot my father's death, but maybe my father was moving quicker on the will and the estate—hence this strange trip to London. All I know is that my brother is not to be trusted. Not at all,—do I make myself clear, Mr. Cleese?"

"Yes, indeed, very clear—do not trust your brother," I said.

I was quite surprised by the information I had just received. Why would Ben sell his brother down the Thames so easily? Was Ben hiding something? Was he trying to send this bloodhound down another path to steer me clear of Ben? I did not know the answers, but I was sure of one thing. *Do not trust either Holmes boy.* "Anything else, Ben, or should we adjourn and rest til morning?" I asked.

"I think I have said enough. I trust you will keep this between us, Mr. Cleese."

"Yes, of course. I will not share this with anyone." Of course I knew that as soon as I saw Hawthorne I would divulge the entire story, but Ben need not know how we detectives solved mysteries. Our lies are worthy, the killer or suspects' lies are not. "Good night, Ben. I will be sure to see you and your brother in the morning," I said.

"Goodnight, William," said Ben.

Ben left quickly but quietly. I went back to reading the paper. I was not all that excited by Ben's information. I already suspected Rex, and I suspected Ben. All Ben had done was to validate my suspicions. As I was starting to read the paper, yet again came a knock at my door. "Who is it now?" I asked heatedly.

"William, let me in, this is Hawthorne."

"Of course, let me grab the door."

"William, I heard you talking in here—was there something I missed?"

"Well, Ben Holmes stopped by and filled me in about why his brother is the murderer and should not be trusted."

"Ha,—why am I not surprised? I am sure you know these brothers are rivals; neither should be trusted. I am sure both wanted the estate for their own gains, and Mr. Holmes had no interest in liquidating his estate. Why else would we be on a journey to London to settle his enigmatic will? These brothers are trouble, aren't they, William?"

"Yes, yes indeed they are, Hawthorne. I knew you would smell their rottenness well before they showed it to us."

"As you know, William, in my years of detective work, I've learned there is one thing true about all killers—they cannot keep their actions a secret. They might not always verbally tell us they killed someone, but their actions tell us exactly what their words do not. Murderers are often narcissists—and narcissists all seek validation. That is why they kill. I think the brothers are really just posturing to protect themselves, but in reality neither is aware of the murderer, because the murderer is not on this train."

"Really? Then where is he?" I asked.

"William, our murderer will reveal himself in London, through the will. Let's get some rest. I am sure tomorrow we will be required to make small talk with these alleged suspects. Good night, William."

"Goodnight, Jack." Hawthorne left as quickly as he came in. I sat down, still puzzled, but rather more interested in reading the paper.

The train ride was a very usual bore. We all got up in the morning, around 6:30 a.m. I met Hawthorne in the dining car around 7. He was already seated and had already ordered his usual poached egg, rye toast, coffee, and swiss cheese.

"Greetings, Hawthorne. How are you this fine morning?" I asked.

"Doing just fine, William. I took the privilege of ordering you a fine breakfast. Eggs, toast, and cheese. I hope you do not mind me taking care of your basic needs," Hawthorne quipped.

"Of course not—the whole meal sounds delicious."

As we began to eat our breakfast the Holmes boys walked in. Ben and Rex quickly came to our table to join us. "Good morning, gents. I hope you are both doing fine this morning," said Rex.

"Yes, we are both enjoying a light breakfast and some coffee. Would you both care for something?" asked Hawthorne.

"Yes, we both would. Waiter, we will have the same as these two, thank you," ordered Rex.

"So, any good news this morning about the state of affairs, Mr. Hawthorne?" asked Rex.

"No, not really. Things seem rather docile at the moment. However, I do expect for things to pick up a bit at the reading of the will, if you know what I mean. I think we are in for an exciting day at St. Paul's Cathedral. Our day will not be filled with the joys and blessings of our righteous Savior; instead I fret to think how the mysteries of this whole murder will send us running around like lost boys, rather than saved souls. Yet I do think the will, with its instructions, will lead us to more knowledge about this killing rather than less. I will say that your father's link to mystic traditions, more importantly the mystic traditions of the Capelli, is very important. I didn't realize this connect until my brother told me he knew Mr. Holmes. For you see, my brother is a third-stage Capelli brother. And the Capelli, unlike the Masons, or, heaven help, us the lunatics of the Illuminati cult, are not interested in uncovering hidden books, or gems, or fabled blood lines or stories. Rather, they wish to understand the mystery of divinity through human flesh. And, like the others who came before them, the brothers stick together, silently, loyally, with adherence to convictions and principles. So when I realized that your father was a Capelli, all of the strange clues began to make sense.

"For example, your father left what appeared to be cryptic numbers on his desk—15:11-32. To the untrained eye the numbers appear random, irrelevant. However, to the trained Capelli eye there is no mistaking the fact that such numbers are clearly bible references. When I considered your father's last word, Luke, the numbers made sense. Luke 15, verses 11 through 32 was where I needed to look. Of course, a student of the bible myself and a believer in the saving power of our Savior, I had a hunch that the bible passage would be a parable, and I was right. The passage is the famous prodigal son moment. Again, a casual reader would be perplexed about the parable; however, to the Capelli order the parable of the prodigal son is the root basis for the existence of the order. The Capelli brothers believed that their calling in life is to return righteously to their father and to ascend between the two worlds of the flesh and the divine. Unlike the mistaken loyal brother in the parable, the Capellis understood, correctly, that the fallen prodigal son's return was the key to divine comprehension. They believed that, just like the prodigal son, man could not understand divinity without also understanding the processes of sin, the falling of man into the world of the flesh, and then the rebirth of man through acknowledging his sins, atoning for his sins, and then baptizing himself anew as saved and freed. Hence, the prodigal son's followers are the Capelli Order."

Rex interrupted, "Okay, but what does my father belonging to the Capelli Order and the mention of the prodigal son have to do with his death?" asked Rex.

"That is a good question. I think your father was clearly telling us that one of you is a prodigal son and one is not. I figure that since you, Rex were rumored to be less motivated by the good intentions and guidance of your father, he saw you as the prodigal son. However, you had not returned home yet, ready to begin anew. Meanwhile, you, Ben, are the loyal son, untrained and ready to join the Capelli Order. Your father had to be confused by the Order's beliefs and his relationships with you both, because he wanted to believe the truth in the Order. He must have been frustrated by knowing that you, Rex, were the prodigal son—though you were not coming home to roost like you should have," said Hawthorne.

"I see. So you think our father was trying to teach Ben and I something about being loyal to him. We could join the Order, if so, and witness something he wanted us to see," asked Rex.

"I think so. I think his death was a move to usher in a change that was necessary for you both to understand and see the power of the Capelli Order. Though I am unsure how these things are connected. Hence, I hope the will and St. Paul's will help us understand. Remember, St. Paul is known as the holder of the keys to divinity. You do not become divine through Paul, but you do come to understand divinity through Paul. A fine Capelli teaching. Hence, your father clearly sent us to St. Paul's to find the key to this puzzle, both his killing and your placement into the Order. To understand the Capelli mind correctly, you must always remember they believed that man and divinity were close to the same thing; the goal in life was to connect the two—just like the prodigal son and father becoming one. I think your father was trying to connect you boys to him. However, it was not working, so in order to usher in the change, something had to happen, which I think is why he was killed," said Hawthorne.

"Well, this is all very interesting, yet confusing," said Ben.

"I know all of this is confusing, but we will learn more through the reading of the will at St. Paul's. The Capellis revered the cathedral, and in such a building as that many clues will avail themselves. Your father is leading us to his killer, amazingly so, from the dead," said Hawthorne.

As Hawthorne finished his coffee and his amazing story about the Capellis, the train stopped. We had arrived at Waterloo station in London. We all moved to grab our belongings and head to the exit. The train came to a slow, screeching stop. We then moved to leave the train. Hawthorne led the way, followed by me and then Lady Holmes and the boys. We all stepped off and waited for Mr. Sidmore. As we turned to look for Mr. Skidmore, Inspector Lewis quickly appeared and moved toward Ben. "Ben Holmes, you are under arrest for the murder of Wendell Holmes. Come with me at once," said Inspector Lewis.

Ben looked shocked. I think we were all shocked. "On what grounds are you arresting him?" asked Hawthorne.

"Jack, we found the poison bottle in Ben's country club jacket, the jacket with the embroidered *B*. We are certain the jacket belongs to Ben," said Lewis.

"Fair enough, Inspector. Even though I think you have the wrong person, the evidence does support an arrest," said Hawthorne.

"Let's go," said Lewis. They took Ben into the police car. We all stood there, amazed, and we wondered if the murder was solved. Yet according to Hawthorne, the murderer was not Ben. So we all turned and looked for Mr. Sidmore to tell us where to head to.

"Ladies and gentlemen, our car awaits. This way, if you please," said Sidmore. We were off to the cathedral. Inspector Lewis escorted Ben. All were hoping we would get to the bottom of this case.

CHAPTER 13

St. Paul's Cathedral

As we drove up the Cathedral I marveled at the brilliance of the building. The cupola of St. Paul's was built to mirror that of her twin cathedral, St. Peter's. In Catholic dogma Paul and Peter are the most critical contributors to the Catholic canon. Paul was the defender and evangelist who spread Christianity throughout the Easter parts of the Empire. Peter held the keys to the Church as the founder and first vicar of Rome. The two men together symbolized the growth and defense of Catholicism.

The building, though majestic, always appears gray and distinct in the London skyline. Unlike the great cathedral in Rome, the one in London had a few minor issues. First, the flying buttresses on the back of the building remind the viewer that the English, unlike the Romans, were not aware of constructing with concrete. Hence St. Paul's is not as stunning or as tall at St. Peter's. And secondly, St. Paul's interior is not nearly as elaborate as St. Peter's—less gold, no amazing alter, much more modest, and much more strangely decorated with symbols from Renaissance Christian times.

We pulled up to the front of the cathedral. Hawthorne and I stared at the impressive building. I knew that Jack had been many times, but as he gazed out of the window, with his broken glasses and sloping gent's hat, he looked very interested at the building—like he was about to learn something new about this ancient masterpiece.

We got out of the car and walked up the pronounced steps to the front gates. Mr. Sidmore led the way, followed by the Holmes family, with us trailing behind. Jack was an old man; he struggled quite noticeably up the stairs. "I am fine, William, no need to treat me like a man entering a nursing home. I will get to the top when I get to the top," shouted Jack.

When we finally reached the top, we both took some deep breaths and then entered the magnificent building. As we entered, I couldn't help notice just how beautiful the front portico of the building was. The front gates were lined in gold trim, and cherubim greeted us from the sides of the gates as we entered. Inside the building the first thing we all noticed was the bright light entering the building from the cupola. The cupola, like so many others, was decorated around its edges with classical Bible stories. The most prominent was the Transfiguration of Christ to heaven.

Mr. Sidmore led us to a small sanctuary where the will reading was to begin, but before we entered Jack stopped to look at something. "William, come here, will you? Look at this small inscription. I think the object appears to be a

Renaissance key. But why would the key be displayed so low to the ground and away from St. Peter, and why would a key be present here at Paul's cathedral?" asked Jack.

"I have no idea. I do know that there are many strange inscriptions inside this building, and scholars are unsure of the meaning. Maybe this is just one of those," I suggested.

"Possibly. I remember as a child coming here for tours, and the tour guide always said the one thing you would never see in this great cathedral is a key symbol, for that is the symbol of Peter, not Paul. Instead, you would find many, many swords and shields, which of course you do find. Never before have I noticed a key, but this placement is certainly hidden. Why do I suppose we will be coming back here, William?" theorized Jack.

"I think your intuition is always getting the better of you, Jack. Let's hurry and meet up with the others."

We made our way into the small sanctuary, which was in the front side, off of the main fornico. The Romans staged their buildings from portico to fornico to the main area, or the salutory. The chapel was called the "magnificent and beloved Mary" sanctuary, a hall dedicated to the unconditional love of the most holy mother of Christ, Mary. Mr. Sidmore took to the front of the room, and the Holmeses sat straight in front. Jack and I, not privy to the reading, sat behind the rest.

"Ladies and gentlemen, thank you for coming. I know this travel has been long, unfortunate, and at times not a luxury, but you are all taking part in the final wishes of your beloved father, husband, and friend, Wendell Holmes. When we drafted his will Wendell made very clear to me that the instructions and administration of the will must take place at St. Paul's Cathedral. He also made certain that since he was a faithful brother of the Capelli order that the details of the will would be left private, only known by him, until the day of his death. As a man of honor, I have respected his wishes and assert to you today I have no knowledge of the details of Mr. Holmes's will. In order to begin the reading, Mr. Holmes instructed that you all take a moment of silence to reflect on your souls and your relationship with the beloved Mary. Please do so," said Mr. Sidmore.

The room fell quiet. Jack and I nodded our heads and silently reflected. I knew I needed to reconcile with Mary and Christ, so I took this time to do so. The Capellis believed that before any great ceremony, the mind, body, and soul must be in communion with Mary and Christ, hence the silent meditation.

"Okay, let's begin with the reading," said Mr. Sidmore. Mr. Sidmore opened a small box that I thought must contain the will. He opened the container, a strange opaque box, and pulled out a shiny object. From the distance we were sitting, the object looked like a configured key, or a key with strange indentations. Mr. Sidmore paused, looked deeper inside, and found a note. "Ladies and gentlemen, let me read this note.

"Greetings, my faithful family, I hope my death and this travel have not inconvenienced you, but in order for my inheritance to be rendered things must take place as a I see fit. As the ancients observed at the time of Christ's death, death is a mystery, and the belongings of life are ever fleeting. As such, my will and inheritance are buried here in St. Paul's. You must go out and find the will. In so doing, you will take part in the legendary old Capelli process of rightful inheritance. The process of finding the will will reveal to you the ancient principles of the order. He who finds the will is clearly of the Capelli order. Now, go out. Remember, the Lord is present, and like a dove he flies overhead looking down on his peaceful children.

"That is all the letter says," said Mr. Sidmore.

Hawthorne started to realize that Wendell Holmes had sent the Holmes family to London and to St. Paul's to teach them about the principles of the Capelli order.

"Oh, come on," sighed Mrs. Holmes. "I am not partaking in a scavenger hunt. Mr. Sidmore, I cannot believe you let Wendell put together this charade. Rex can assist you in finding the will; I will wait here. Possibly Mr. Hawthorne could assist," she speculated.

"Yes, of course. I think finding this will will also indicate the killer to us. So I gladly will take part," said Jack.

So off we went. "The final part of the letter said the Lord is present and he is like a dove, so I think we must go to the cupola and find the exact spot in the Transfiguration painting where the dove is and where Christ is pointing or looking to," said Hawthorne to everyone. So we all quickly moved to the center of the cathedral. There above was the Transfiguration painting of Christ, very similar to Rafael's in Rome. Christ appeared in all white, a dove above his right shoulder; Christ did not look at the dove. Instead he pointed slightly off to the right from the white dove. "See there, Christ's finger is pointing just off to the right of the dove in the direction of the fourth row in the balcony. I say we head up there for the next clue," said Hawthorne.

We all scampered up the stairs to the balcony, fourth row, and there was another box, with a small key hole. Mr. Sidmore took the key and opened the box. "Bingo, Hawthorne, spot on—you are good at this hunt."

Mr. Sidmore opened the box, and inside awaited another clue, written on white cloth. "Now that you are reminded of the purity of Christ in peace and height, go find the weeping mother, who cared so much for her son that she could not bear but to look away at the time of his death."

Clearly that is the Pieta, but that is in Rome, thought Hawthorne. *Unless maybe there is another painting here in St. Paul's of Mary weeping at the Cross at Cavalry, but where is it?* "Let's go downstairs and look around for this mysterious painting."

We moved back down to the sanctuary for Mary, where Lady Holmes had remained after we left. Hawthorne figured the painting had to be somewhere in the sanctuary. So we all scrambled around the sanctuary looking for the painting. I went directly toward the praying alter, and Hawthorne moved towards the statue of Mary.

"Gents, over here," said Mr. Sidmore. "I think have found it here behind this painting by Drurer, I think." Mr. Sidmore had found Albrecht Drurer's most famous painting, the Melancholy. Modern Christians had probably never heard of the famous painting, but it was a prevalent painting in the mid-to-late-Middle Ages among mystic Christians of Europe. The painting depicted a melancholy angel who sat sad-faced, his wings pointing down, his head hanging low, his sword and shield falling off his lap, surrounded by other cherubim who were equally unhappy. The painting for mystics depicted the fallen and failed attempt of the divine to reach the souls of mortal men and how failing to do so led to heartbreak among the angels. Other mystics saw more mystery in the painting because of unusual numeric grids in the painting, though they more or less felt that the painting depicted the failure of man to become divine unless man was encouraged through divine intervention. Hence, some mystics took the meaning of the painting to be a signal from God to reach out to the ancient angelic order and to summon their graces. Then man would be rejoined with the chorus of angels and would move closer to divinity.

To the left of the Drurer painting was the even more odd painting from the great Michelangelo, the painting of Mary, on her knees, head covered, weeping at the base of the Christ's cross at Cavalry. Most modern Christians would simply look at such a painting and conclude that Mary was heartbroken over the loss of her son, but ancient to Renaissance Christians understood the true meaning of the painting, which was that Mary was not weeping for the loss of her son but for the loss of mankind from losing her son. Ancient mystics believed that Mary understood that Christ's death on the Cross would leave many Christians to believe that the revelation of God was complete and that Christians should just follow Christ to heaven. Rather, the ancients believed that the death on the Cross meant the new world order of Christendom had begun on Earth, not just in heaven. Mary was kneeling at the Cross because the loss of her son symbolized the loss of Christ on Earth and the struggle that man would now have in creating a righteous earthly Christian kingdom. Hence, many ancient Christians would pray to Mary, asking her to bring them closer to Christ in earthly fashion so they could usher in a new Christian kingdom. The weeping was a constant reminder of what "fallen" man had done to the righteous King and how his righteous mother cried for all of mankind. The mystics believed in correcting this wrong by becoming Christ-like and by creating a Christian kingdom on Earth.

The Capelli Order understood the painting to symbolize the fallen nature of man away from God, and Mary was incarnate of God weeping for the loss of mankind. Hence the painting was significant to the Capelli Order because sons were never to betray their mothers; in so doing, they were betraying the righteous Mother of God.

"Look here!" exclaimed Hawthorne. "There is another note." Jack opened the note.

> "Now that you understand fallen man's despise for both God and our earthly mother, you must understand that man has never touched the Hand of God since. Not because he is incapable of doing so, but because man has betrayed his Father, and Mother. In order to find the lock to open my will, you must

come to terms with the galactic struggle between betrayal and righteousness."

Hawthorne looked puzzled.

Galactic battle between betrayal and righteousness, he thought.

"I know that the Capelli order was disposed of defending the honor of fraternity by correcting the betrayal of Christ and Mary, by mankind. However, what does the galactic battle between betrayal and righteousness have to do with his murder? Clearly, staring at the Transfiguration, coupled with the weeping Mother Mary, tells us that Wendell felt he was trying to cleanse someone, and that he was betrayed just like the weeping Mary, but who and how? Wendell was betrayed, wept to cleanse the sins of the betrayer, but is his death the attempt to correct the wrong and to provide atonement?" said Hawthorne.

"I have no idea, but I do remember an ancient story about one constellation, Orion, fending off the raging ram, which was to symbolize God's anger over man's constant need to defeat divine righteousness, instead of man defeating his own sins—the raging ram. Orion was God trying to shield man from the unwanted nature of desires and wretchedness, the raging ram."

"You are right, William. We need to find Orion's constellation, here at St. Paul's. I can't recall ever seeing such a rendering of the constellation. Unless, of course, we look for staccato markings in the stone construction; then maybe we would find the vague constellation. Never would someone think to line up staccato markings. Yet what a perfect way to hide a meaning of importance in such a highly visible building. Come, we must move to the cupola and start connecting staccato markings. I think doing so will lead us to Orion, which will lead us to the death of Wendell Holmes," Hawthorne said.

The ancient mystic Christians believed that the Orion constellation was the only constellation that God placed in the heavenly sky to remind man about the divine war between righteousness and sin. Orion symbolized God fending off sin, which was symbolized by the raging bull, or the constellation Taurus. Inside the Orion constellation is the star Betelgeuse, which mystics believed was the mark of Satan himself. Many ancients prayed and believed that the day of divine righteousness would come and be visible when Orion had defeated Taurus. Hence many great objects were built aligned with Orion's belt: the pyramids at Giza, Stonehenge, and the temple of Machu Picchu—they all understood that the constellation was much more than a gathering of stars. Instead, the constellation was a message from God: if you turn from sin, you will defeat the raging bull in you, and you will become more divine and righteous.

"Let's start looking," said Hawthorne. Hawthorne, in his mind, was beginning to piece together the murder. He now understood that Wendell Holmes was a member of the Capelli order, a Christian mystic order, and he understood that Wendell had sent them to St. Paul's to reveal to them, or someone, about the principles of the order—mainly loyalty, sacrifice, and redemption. The story of the Orion constellation evidenced the Capelli belief that all men must reject their carnal temptations so they can be redeemed.

Hawthorne was confused, though, by who Wendell was trying to save, and from what sin.

After a few minutes Hawthorne had discovered the pattern that connected the staccato together, revealing the Orion Constellation. Of course the belt was most significant, and Hawthorne quickly saw how the belt, taken out of the constellation, represented a shaped arrow that pointed directly at a small stone box sitting to the right of the cathedral's main alter. There lay the lock to Holmes's will.

Hawthorne was eager to go to the box, but reluctant at the same time. "Hold up a minute, William," he said. "I think we need to think about this murder before we open up the box, because someone here might be interested in harming us once we open the box. Remember that Rex Holmes stands to inherit a ton of money, unless, of course, his father has altered the will. If his father altered the will, which I have reason to think he did, then Rex might become hostile before and after opening the will. We have to ask ourselves what the meaning of the Orion constellation and Wendell's death is. What is Wendell trying to tell us?" said Hawthorne. "Further, William, I think Wendell believed that one of his sons had betrayed him, just like the story of the prodigal son. I think Wendell also believed that he was to teach one of his sons a lesson about sacrifice and redemption. Hence the Orion constellation and the raging bull symbols—but is Rex or Ben the son that Wendell is trying to redeem?" said Hawthorne.

I interrupted. "Well, we know that Wendell was a brother in the Capelli Order, we know that the Capelli brothers were mystics who believed in the divinity of Mary, coupled with the divinity of Christ. We know that the Capelli order also believed that many of life's mysteries were revealed to man through the constellations, and the Orion constellation is the significant story of the bull, Taurus, being fended off by the bravery of Orion," I said.

"Yes, William you are right about that. We know that the Church ordered the Capellis to disband for their worship of Mary. Maybe that is why Wendell brought us to St. Paul's Cathedral. Paul was a convert who had a revelation and converted from Judaism to Christianity. The Capelli brothers had converted from traditional Christianity to a mystic form of Mary and Christ worship. Wendell had us start in the temple for Mary, clearly telling us to adore her and to worship her, but what else was he saying about his murder? Was he trying to tell us something about his own family in taking us here and reminding us of the weeping Mary? Who was Wendell weeping for?" said Hawthorne.

"That's it. Remember the night before the murder, the help overheard Wendell arguing on the phone. The person on the other end is the person he was weeping for. Imagine if Mary had a conversation with Christ the night before his death. She probably would have pleaded with him to not go through with it. So maybe Wendell was pleading with someone not to go through with something very important to him—like the ownership of the business. Remember that his eldest son Rex did not want to run the business; he wanted to sell the business. Well, what if Wendell had decided to change the will and not give Rex the business? And what if Rex was trying to take the business from his father? Remember when Rex told us about how foggy and confused his father had become? Ahh, I see now. I see what is going on here," said Hawthorne.

"The Taurus is Rex—the raging bull symbolizes a sinner who wants to destroy—in this case the family business. Orion is who?" said Hawthorne.

"Well, Orion could be Rex, but what would he gain by killing his father, unless the will was already changed?" I asked.

"Exactly, William. Nothing would be gained," said Hawthorne.

"Maybe then the killer is Ben, who is already in custody. The police did find the canister that contained the poison in Ben's coat pocket," I said.

"Only a complete idiot would indict himself. Clearly Ben was framed, or mistakenly framed," said Hawthorne. "I think the reading of the will is actually going to tell us about the killer. This murder, like so many others, William, is a killing of passion, love, and tragedy. Come, we need to have the will read," said Hawthorne.

We scampered over to the place next to the stone box where everyone had gathered. Mr. Sidmore, the family attorney held the golden key in his left hand and the stone box in his right. "I suppose we must open this now," he said. He slowly turned the key in the key hole and opened the box. I was now feeling the suspense of the moment. Hawthorne seemed intrigued, and Rex Holmes stared endlessly at the box. Lady Holmes sat quietly, with little reverence.

"Let's see what is inside," said Mr. Skidmore. He pulled out a very short piece of paper. Mr. Skidmore then proceeded to read the paper aloud.

> "Dear family, friends, and Mr. Hawthorne. I have gathered you in this great cathedral to pay my last respects to you, my family, and to my brothers in the Capelli Order. I leave my entire estate to my youngest son, Ben, and my wife Lady, to be shared equally."

That was the end of the letter. Everyone thought it was strange that Mr. Hawthorne's name was included in the greeting.

Lady Holmes was anxiously relieved, but Rex Holmes kicked his feet to the ground. "What on earth did my father do? He cannot leave the estate to my brother and mother. My brother is incapable of running or selling this business. This is outrageous, wasting all of this time to learn this," said Rex.

"Mr. Hawthorne, do you have anything to say?" asked Lady Holmes.

"My dear Lady Holmes, I must say this whole affair has perplexed me from the very beginning. Here we have the most unfortunate death of your beloved husband. A man who on a simple Sunday morning ended up dead, clearly poisoned by the planting of something into his morning coffee. Well, the only people around that morning were you and Ms. Mary Margaret—but what reason would either of you have to kill Wendell? Especially in light of the will, I can see no clear reason why either of you would kill Wendell.

Ms. Mary recalls a violent phone exchange, so neither of you were on the other end of that phone call, and I knew neither of you had anything to do with this death. But, strangely, I think you, Lady Holmes, know who the killer is. After all, how would you surmise the poison got in Wendell's cup if you or Mary did not put it there?" asked Hawthorne.

"Whatever do you mean?" said Lady Holmes. "I have no clue by who or how Wendell was killed. I have made that point many times."

"You have told me some things, Lady Holmes, but not everything. When I first met you the day after the death, you did not seem very upset about your husband's death. In fact, you were busily planning a social event for the end of the week. You were distraught but seemed irritated as well by the murder. I found such behavior odd, but I wrote off the peculiarity to a quirky personality. However, looking back now, I think the reason you were not very distressed by the death is because you knew about the murder and the murderer all along, didn't you?" asked Hawthorne.

"Stop berating my mother," interrupted Rex. "She already told you she knew nothing about any of this."

"Ahh, Rex Holmes, the eldest son who wanted to sell his father's pearl, the family business. I suspected you from the very beginning of all of this. You had the most to gain or lose with your father's passing. The will now reveals all of what you lost, though. Your father sent us here to teach or tell you something. But what was he telling? The symbolism is interesting. First, we have the weeping Mary, the most sacred of beings to a mystic Capelli; then we have the Orion constellation and the repelling of Taurus. What does this all mean? Who was Wendell weeping for? And who is the raging bull or sinner? I thought about these questions for some time, and then of course, like all great puzzles, the answer came to me. Rex, you are the raging bull. Your father is weeping for you to turn away from your devious behavior toward the Order. However, you opposed him. Hence the phone call the night before his murder. Wendell saw himself as Orion trying to hold you off, but how could he hold you back? You had decided to take over the business whether your father agreed or not. Hence, Wendell had one last option. He could sacrifice himself for the family business. Wendell bought the poison, tainted his own coffee that morning, and then waited to die. Remember the hexagon note and the scribbled Latin phrases on his desk. At first I could not figure out what Wendell was trying to tell us, but the most striking message was right in front of our eyes. Semper Fidelis—always faithful. Wendell was faithful to family, business, and the Capelli Order. To protect the business he had to stop you, and likewise to protect the family he had to stop you. To reveal to you the importance of the Order he sent you on this hunt for the will. He did all of this to save you, Rex, from yourself. Your father was both weeping and saving you from your sins—he was a very true Capelli to the very end. There is no murder here. Instead, my dear friends, this is a case of tragedy, betrayal, sadness, and suicide. I am sorry to tell you this," said Hawthorne.

Everyone stood stunned for a while. Lady Holmes wept, but she already knew that Wendell had done this. She had feared his senility was depressing him, and his fear of Rex taking over the family business was making him desperate. She was amazed at how well Hawthorne had pieced everything together. Rex stood saddened but arrogantly appalled at his father's actions. Ben, of course, was relieved.

"Well, I suppose my business here is done," said Hawthorne. "William will please help me back to the car. I want out of dreary London at once. I hope all of you have a safe trip back home. I am headed to Westbury for some relaxation."

As was Hawthorne's personal way, he tended to act very opaque after solving a crime, as if everyone would be like him and just move on past the horror of the realizations. He would move quickly, easily, and readily on to the next task of life. "Well, William, are you coming or not? asked Hawthorne. He held up his broken glasses, punched his willowing hat, and smiled. "Solving a crime never gets old, instead I just get old," he chuckled. "Come on, I need something to eat, and the hour is growing long. This matter is done, and that means so are we. Hurry along, William. You never know when I am going to be needed again, or where, so let's head back to Westbury."

As they walked out to a waiting car, I could not help but wonder about the suicide of Wendell Holmes. "Hawthorne, I am often confused by murder, and this one is clearly confusing. I just find the whole suicide lacks logic. If Wendell wanted to protect the family, then why not kill Rex? Why would Wendell think that by killing himself, he would save the family and teach Rex a moral lesson about sacrifice, redemption, and loyalty?" I asked.

Hawthorne turned back to me to speak. "You see, William, the one thing you must know about murder, killing, or suicide is that the actions of a killer are never logical. Criminal behavior is always irrational. I think Mr. Holmes thought that his time was growing short, so to protect the family business he had to do something hastily. He could not trust Rex, so he decided to kill himself, after revising the will, to prohibit any chance of Rex receiving the inheritance. But further, I think Wendell really wanted to save his son from his bad choices, and Wendell must have thought that in order to reveal the principles of sacrifice, redemption, and loyalty to his son, the only way was to do something drastic—hence Wendell sacrificed himself to reveal to his son Rex the importance of sacrifice, redemption, and loyalty. Will Rex understand this message? Maybe, maybe not. The only truth in all of this tragedy is death—and death, my friend, is never truly logical, nor truly understood. Come now. We must head to Westbury," said Hawthorne.

I was still confused. I realized maybe I was incapable of comprehending the moral lesson that Wendell had intended for Rex. Sacrifice is hard to comprehend.